VICTOR AND THE BUNGLERS IN SPACE
OUT TO LUNCH

written by Jimmy Hibbert
illustrated by Primary Design

Carnival
An Imprint of HarperCollins*Publishers*

Victor and Hugo of Naughtiness
International were up to no good as usual.
Arriving outside a bank, armed with a
banana and a cucumber, Victor had been
sure that this time nothing would go wrong.

"Are you ready?" he hissed to his brother.
"Ready, my Victor!" replied Hugo.
"Then let's go!"

The people in the bank were certainly
surprised when the two burst out of their
van. Victor shouted, "Don't anybody make
the movies and nobody will..." but before he
could finish what he was about to say, he
felt Hugo tugging at his tie.

"Let go of my tie, you buffless foonbrain!" snorted Victor.

"You mean brainless buffoon," corrected Hugo.

"Yes. That is what I said," lied Victor. "What do you want?"

"Look!" said Hugo, and he pointed to a camera on the wall. "We are on television!"

"You fool! That is the ..." Victor's words fell on deaf ears. He was going to explain that the camera was part of the bank's security video system but it was too late – Hugo had launched into a song and dance routine.

"Hee hee!" he confided to Victor, tap-dancing madly. "Soon I will be a star, yes?"

"Soon you will have the bump on the head!" snarled Victor. But before he could carry out his threat, he realised that they were being watched by three very large, very fierce and very angry security guards. Victor knew when he was beaten and so, picking Hugo up by the scruff of the neck, he ran for the door.

"Hey!" protested Hugo. "I hadn't finished!"

"We will both be finished if you do not come along," said Victor.

The two brothers charged out of the bank and straight into a van full of policemen who had been alerted to the bank raid.

"There they are!" cried a rather portly police sergeant. "After them!" and he and his companions leapt out of their van to give chase to the two would-be bank robbers.

"Aaaagh!" screamed Victor.

"Help! It is the police!" said Hugo. For once in his life he was right. Taking to their heels, they raced back to the safety of their van.

"Step on it!" Victor shouted, slamming the door.

"Yes Victor. Stepping on it right away... erm... what is it that you want me to step on?"

"I mean drive!" Victor was getting hysterical. "Drive, you fool!"

"Ah! I see! Then why did you not say so?"

"I did say... just DRIVE!!!"

Hugo started the van, put it into gear and accelerated. Unfortunately he had put the van into reverse, and he and Victor were now backing at speed towards the approaching policemen.

"You idiot!" screamed Victor. "Not backwards! Forwards! Forwards!"

The speeding van scattered the pursuing policemen, all except for the sergeant, who was not as quick as he used to be. The van ran over his size 13 boot. He screamed and hopped about in the road clutching his injured foot.

Hugo brought the van to a halt and found the right gear; the van shot forward and ran over the sergeant's other size 13 boot. The sergeant soon found out that you cannot hold both feet at the same time and stay upright. He landed with a heavy bump on his bottom in the middle of the road.

"Well, don't just stand there!" he shouted at the others. "Get after them!"

Some time later, having shaken off their pursuers, Hugo brought the van to a halt outside a park.

"Why are you stopping?" Victor asked.

"Penelope says that she would like a little walk in the park," said Hugo, taking a matchbox from his pocket and looking in it.

"I don't care about your stupid, stupid pet earwig," said Victor, cruelly.

"Victor!" Hugo gasped.

"What about those big policemen who are searching the town for us."

"What policemen?" asked Hugo, looking around.

"The policemen who chased us after you ruined the bank robbery, you dunderhead!" Victor sighed a deep sigh. "Now we will have to find a place to hide until the heat has died down."

"Perhaps you should take your vest off then, Victor," suggested Hugo, helpfully.

"My... my vest? What has my vest got to do with anything?" Victor was puzzled.

"You said you were hot..." explained Hugo.

"No I did not!" Victor exploded.

"Ooh Victor. You are a fibber! I heard you! You said..."

"Yes, well, it does not matter now. What matters now is... aha!" Across the road Victor had spotted a restaurant called *The Happy Frog*. There was a notice in the window.

"What matters is... aha?" It was Hugo's turn to be puzzled.

"Wanted: waiting staff. Enquire within," chuckled Victor.

"I do not understand, Victor," frowned Hugo. "First you say what matters is aha, and now you say you want a staff that is waiting."

"Hugo," Victor spoke through gritted teeth. "Hugo, you will please listen to me!"

"Yes, Victor. I will listen. I will listen very carefully. I will listen with both of my ears. I will listen with this ear," he said, holding out his left ear for Victor to see, "and I will also listen with this ear as well," he continued, holding his other ear. "I will listen with..."

Victor had had enough. "Silence, be quiet, shush, shut up and...and...shut up!" he raged. "I said 'Aha' because I have had an idea. And I have had the idea when I read the notice that I have seen in the restaurant window...;

"They want waiters. We will be the waiters! The policemen will not be looking for waiters. They will be looking for two famous international criminals and a van. Ha! It is a good idea is it not, Hugo?" Victor was very pleased with himself, but Hugo said nothing.

"Hugo? It is a good idea, yes?" Still Hugo said nothing.

"Hugo! You will please answer me!" Victor was getting quite cross.

11

"Well, make up your mind!" sulked Hugo. "First you say to shut up, and then you get angry when I do!"

Victor, eager to carry out his plan, bounded out of the van. "Well?" he said, "What are you waiting for? Come along."

"Oh... all right." Hugo followed Victor into restaurant.

The owner of *The Happy Frog*, Mr Francois, was busy setting the tables for lunch. He wore a white jacket, check trousers and a huge chef's hat.

"Bonjour, Monsieur!" beamed Victor as he and a still sulky Hugo entered the dining room. "We are the waiters that you are requesting."

"And by your accent, I would say that you are French as well!" Mr Francois was delighted.

"But yes! As French as two French beans!"

"Well," said Mr Francois, a man used to making quick decisions, "I shall take you on one week's trial."

"Thank you, Monsieur!" Victor bowed low in front of their new employer. "We will not let you down."

"I hope not," said Mr Francois, "Now. Let me show you the kitchens." He went towards some double doors at the rear of the dining room. "Walk this way."

"If I could walk that way, I'd have my knees on inside out!" giggled Hugo.

"What was that?" Mr Francois turned to face his two new waiters.

"Nothing, Monsieur! Nothing at all!" replied Victor, snatching Hugo's beret from his head and stuffing it in his brother's mouth.

"Gwfffmngng!" said Hugo.

"Heh heh heh!" Victor's laugh sounded a little strained. "My brother – he always likes a little snack at about this time…"

Mr Francois eyed Victor with suspicion, but made no comment.

The kitchen was quite large. It was equipped with gleaming copper saucepans, spoons and ladles, knives of all sizes and every kitchen implement imaginable, from melon scoops to garlic crushers. Giant pots bubbled and steamed on the huge stoves and delicious aromas filled the air. Mr Francois walked along the kitchen range, giving a little stir here and adding a touch of seasoning there.

Mr Francois pointed to two waiters' outfits hanging on a peg. "There are your uniforms," he said. "Put them on. We shall be opening in fifteen minutes."

Moments later Victor and Hugo were smartly dressed in long, white aprons over white shirts with black bow ties and black trousers. The fact that Hugo still had his beret in his mouth rather spoiled the effect. Victor removed it and replaced it soggily on Hugo's head.

Mr Francois clucked with approval. "You'll do – now to work!"

On the stroke of opening time in walked a very large man with his equally large wife, who wore a large hat decked with very colourful artificial flowers.

"Good afternoon Monsieur, Madame!" smiled Victor.

"Table for two, my good man," said the man in a rather blubbery voice.

"You think that will be big enough?" Hugo joked.

"I beg your pardon?!" the fat man said.

"Nothing, Monsieur! He said nothing!" Victor said hurriedly. "If you would care to be seated here, I will fetch the menu." Victor showed the couple to a table and clicked his fingers. "Hugo!" he said. "The menu!"

"The men who what?" Hugo asked.

"Not the men who, the menu! The menu! The list of the food!" Victor said angrily.

"Ah! Well, why didn't you say so?" replied Hugo, and he went to fetch two menus.

"I did say… oh just give them to me!" said Victor, snatching the menus from his brother with such force that he knocked the woman's hat off.

"OUCH!" she screamed.

"What the devil do you think you're doing?" Her husband had gone quite red and he was quivering with indignation.

"Heh heh heh. So sorry. A little accident. It will not happen again!" said Victor.

"I should jolly well think not!" The man calmed down and took a menu, licking his lips wetly as he read it.

Just then another customer came into the restaurant – a thin man with a sharp nose and a pair of gold rimmed spectacles. He sat by himself in a corner and started to make little notes in a book. Victor took him a menu which he glanced at quickly, making another note in his little book.

"Waiter!" shouted the fat man, and Victor went over to his table.

"Monsieur?" enquired Victor.

"We're ready to order. Do you have frogs' legs?"

Victor gave him a withering look. "No, Monsieur. It must be the way I walk," he said sarcastically.

"Is that supposed to be a joke?" thundered the man. In the corner, the man with spectacles continued to scribble away.

"No Monsieur, it is not," replied Victor with dignity. "And please do not make the remarks about my legs."

"I wasn't; I..."

"I'll have the soup," said his wife, hoping to avoid a nasty scene. "Followed by the spaghetti bolognese, please."

"Harrumph. Well, I'll take the soup as well," said the fat man. "And then the chicken."

"Yes, Monsieur, Madame," said Victor. He walked to the kitchen to deliver the order.

Hugo, meanwhile, was attending to the man with the notebook. "Can you recommend the braised duckling?" he asked in a nasal voice that reminded Hugo of the sound the bath water makes as it goes down the plug-hole. Hugo wasn't quite sure what he meant, but he thought it best to say yes. So he did.

"Yes. Oh yes. Yes, yes, yes!" In fact he overdid it a bit.

"Yes, I get the general idea, thank you," said the man, and wrote something else in his little book. "And to start with I shall have snails."

Hugo looked at the man. He blinked. He shook his head and wiggled a finger in his ear to make sure he had heard right.

"You will have what?" he asked in disbelief.

"Snails." Yes. That was what Hugo thought the man had said.

"Snails?!?" He couldn't believe his ears. "You mean the creepy crawly things with the pointy feelers and the shells, that are all slimy and slow and..."

"Yes! Snails! I'd like half a dozen, please."
The man looked down at his notebook,
ending the conversation.

Snails! The man must be mad, thought
Hugo, feeling rather queasy. Snails! Well, if
that was what he wanted...

Victor came back into the dining room
with two bowls of soup for the fat man and
his wife, just in time to see Hugo nipping
out of the front door.

"Hugo?" he shouted. "Where are you
going?" But Hugo was already out of
earshot, walking through the gate of the
park opposite the restaurant.

"Typical!" thought Victor, serving the soup. "It is always I who have to do everything!"

The fat man scowled at his soup bowl and pointed an accusing finger. "Waiter? What is this fly doing in my soup?"

Victor peered closely. "Hmmmn, it looks to me like it is trying to swim out of the..."

"Take it away! And bring me another bowl. This time, without the fly!" The fat man looked as if he might explode, so Victor took his bowl back into the kitchen.

While he was gone, Hugo arrived back in the dining room and ran straight over to the man with the notebook.

"I am sorry, Monsieur. I could not find any snails. So I have brought instead some slugs and a few worms." He emptied his pockets. Several large, plump and very slimy slugs plopped on to the spotless white table cloth together with three very long, pink worms.

The man with the notebook looked horrified. His face turned the colour of uncooked pastry. "This is monstrous! Quite monstrous!" he cried.

"No, no. It is some slugs and some worms," Hugo corrected him.

"I'll have you know, I am an inspector for the good food guide and I have never..." (here the man stood up, knocking the table over in his anger) "NEVER been treated like this!" He advanced upon Hugo who backed away from him towards the kitchen doors.

It was unfortunate that Victor should have chosen just this moment to return from the kitchen with the soup. Hugo backed into him and Victor tripped, letting go of the bowl. Up through the air it sailed and down it came, landing with a wet splat on the fat lady's hat.

Her husband sprang to his feet, knocking his chair backwards through the restaurant window. As he marched towards Victor in a fury, he failed to notice that one of the slugs had slithered into his path. He put his foot on it and wheee! he shot across the dining room, through the double doors into the kitchen.

The sound from the kitchen was colossal. There were bangs and crashes. There were splashes and squelches. There were screams and shouts. There were clangs, clatters, clunks and pings. Then the doors burst open and Mr Francois came out.

"What is going on here!" he screamed. He was covered from head to toe in sauce, soup, stew, gravy, greens, spaghetti and chips, and his chef's hat stood at a crazy angle on his head. A pea dropped out of his ear and rolled across the floor.

The man with the notebook spoke up. "Your restaurant is the worst place I have ever had to inspect, Mr Francois. Not only is the service appalling…"

But before he could finish, there came a yelp and a growl. "Oh no…" breathed Victor, screwing up his eyes. Suddenly, from nowhere, a little dog ran into the restaurant. It shot up Victor's trouser leg and down the other, removing Victor's underpants on the way.

"Yeeeowwrgh!" screeched Victor.

"…and I see you also keep pets on the premises," continued the man, making yet more notes.

Mr Francois glowered at Victor and Hugo. "Well?" he demanded.

"Monsieur, I can explain everything," said Victor.

He thought for a second, then a second more. "No," he decided. "I cannot... Hugo?"

"Yes Victor?" answered his brother.

"RUN!!!" shouted Victor. And run they did. Straight into the arms of a police sergeant with very sore feet who had come to investigate the noise.

"All right, all right. What's... " The police sergeant stopped and blinked. "Just a minute – I recognise you! You're the two what ran over me feet this morning!"

"There must be some mistake," said Victor, lamely.